WEE LITTLE
LAMB

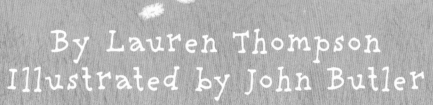

By Lauren Thompson
Illustrated by John Butler

Simon & Schuster Books for Young Readers
New York   London   Toronto   Sydney

It was spring in the meadow,
and the wee little lamb
was all brand-new.

This wee little lamb
was a shy little lamb.

"Won't you say hello?"
asked the flouncy pouncy rabbit.

But the wee little lamb
just hid behind his mama.

"Come jump with all my friends!"
chirped the cheery crickety cricket.

But the wee little lamb
just hid behind his mama.

"Sing a song with me!"
trilled the jolly robin redbreast.

But the wee little lamb
would sing only with his mama.

"Come see the great, wide world!"
called the swooping old hoot owl.

But the wee little lamb
stayed right beside his mama.

Then a tiny voice peeped,
"Will you play with me?"
It was a bitty little mouse
peeking round her bitty mama!

The lamb softly said,
"Yes, I'll play with you!"

Then the wee little lamb
and the bitty little mouse
played right beside their mamas!

what fun!

TO CHARLOTTE—L. T.
FOR IAN—J. B.

SIMON & SCHUSTER BOOKS FOR YOUNG READERS
An imprint of Simon & Schuster Children's Publishing Division
1230 Avenue of the Americas, New York, New York 10020
Text copyright © 2009 by Lauren Thompson
Illustrations copyright © 2009 by John Butler
SIMON & SCHUSTER BOOKS FOR YOUNG READERS is a trademark of Simon & Schuster, Inc.
Book design by Lucy Ruth Cummins and Laurent Linn
The text for this book is set in Neutra Text.
The illustrations for this book are rendered in acrylic paint and colored pencils.
Manufactured in China
2 4 6 8 10 9 7 5 3 1
Library of Congress Cataloging-in-Publication Data
Thompson, Lauren.
Wee little lamb / Lauren Thompson ; illustrated by John Butler.—1st ed.
p.   cm.
Summary: A little, newborn lamb, too shy to say hello to the rabbit or
sing with the robin, is finally drawn out by a tiny field mouse.
ISBN-13: 978-1-4169-3469-1
ISBN-10: 1-4169-3469-3
[1. Bashfulness—Fiction. 2. Sheep—Fiction. 3. Mice—Fiction.
4. Animals—Infancy—Fiction.] I. Butler, John, 1952- ill. II. Title.
PZ7.T37163Wee 2009   [E]—dc22   2008004428